Goodbye, Walter Malinski

Goodbye, Walter Malinski

Helen Recorvits

Pictures by Lloyd Bloom

Frances Foster Books

Farrar, Straus and Giroux • *New York*

Distributed in Canada by Douglas & McIntyre Ltd.
Printed and bound in the United States of America
Designed by Judith M. Lanfredi
First edition, 1999
3 5 7 9 10 8 6 4 2

Library of Congress Cataloging-in-Publication Data

Recorvits, Helen.
    Goodbye, Walter Malinski/Helen Recorvits; pictures by Lloyd Bloom
    —1st ed.
        p. cm.
    Summary: In 1934, even though life is hard for Wanda Malinski and
her family, she enjoys school, good times with her best friend, and a special
relationship with her older brother.
    ISBN 0-374-32747-5
    [1. Brothers and sisters—Fiction.   2. Family life—Fiction.
3. Depressions—1929—Fiction.   4. Death—Fiction.   5. Polish Americans—
Fiction.]   I. Bloom, Lloyd, ill.   II. Title.
    PZ7.R24435Go 1999
    [Fic]—dc21   97-35451

In memory of my grandmother
Francziska Czupryna

Contents

Goodbye, Walter Malinski

1
Fireside Chat

We were sitting around the radio, listening to President Roosevelt's Fireside Chat. The President was talking about something called the CCC. The Civilian Conservation Corps. It was for young people who couldn't find jobs. Pa got real excited.

"You! You! You're going!" Pa pointed his finger at my brother, Walter. "You'll give us your pay, and we can all eat a little better. You're going!"

Walter stared down at the floor. I couldn't tell what he was thinking. Even if he liked the idea, I couldn't tell. Walter hardly ever let on how he felt about anything.

"CCC? What's that? What?" Ma asked. She wasn't good with English.

"It's jobs! It's government jobs for boys," Pa said in Polish. "They teach you how to build houses. You plant trees, help fight fires, all kinds of jobs. You live at a camp. They give you food and money."

"At a camp?" Ma said. "I don't like that idea. Sounds like the army to me."

"But, Pa, Walter's not old enough," my sister Victoria said. "You have to be eighteen years old. Walter is only fifteen."

"They'll never know," Pa said. "They give you food and money. Walter's going!"

"Sounds like the army to me!" Ma said.

"Aah! You! What do you know!" Pa said.

Well, we all knew we were poor. It hadn't always been like this. In the good days, Pa used to work in the dye house. He made dye for the cloth at Harrington's Cotton Mill, and he used to work long hours. We had enough money for shoes and clothes. We had meat for supper almost every day, and sometimes there was money left over for ice-cream cones. We'd all take a walk down to the drugstore, and Pa would tell us jokes he heard at work. He'd make us all laugh.

"Knock, knock," Pa would say.

"Who's there?"

"Olive."

"Olive who?"

"Olive you!"

The drugstore had one of those new pinball machines. Sometimes Pa would let Walter and me each have a turn. A turn cost a whole nickel. Those were the days when we had nickels to spare. Pa used to be fun.

But times were bad now. The cotton mill and the dye house laid off a lot of workers, and Pa was one of the unlucky ones. He tried to get a job at one of the other mills in town, but no one was hiring. Many mills had gone out of business. Pa could talk some English, and he was a hard worker. It didn't matter. There were no jobs. There were no more jokes and no more ice-cream cones.

Now Pa took walks by himself past all the closed mills. Ma always had tea waiting for him at home, and they'd talk together. "What's going to happen to us?" he'd say, sighing.

Sometimes Pa's cousin Chester, who lived in Greenville, would hire Pa to help out on his farm. It wasn't a big farm, and Chester didn't really need much help. It was far, too—about eight miles away. Pa walked there and back, but he didn't complain. He took the work when he could get it.

"We're still luckier than others," Victoria told me. "Some people in other parts of the country are standing in lines for bread, and they eat at soup kitchens. Some people are homeless. At least we have a place to live."

I got scared when Victoria said that. We were living in one of the row houses owned by the cotton mill.

"What if the Harringtons made us find another place to live? Would we have to beg on the street?" I asked.

Victoria tried to cheer me up. "Listen to me, Wanda Malinski! Things will get better for us. You'll see. Any day now, Pa will get a job."

"What's going to happen to us?" I sighed.

As the weeks went by that fall of 1934, Pa talked more and more about the Civilian Conservation Corps. Chester knew some people downtown who worked for the city. Pa and Chester were going to fix things so Walter could go.

Sometimes Walter seemed to get a little interested. "CCC sounds good to me. They'll give me good shoes, and I'll eat three meals a day. Big meals, too! Ham, roast beef, even lamb."

"But, Walter, you don't like lamb," I reminded him.

"I'll like it. I'll build houses and make roads. That's real men's work!"

"But, Walter!"

"What? What?" he asked me.

"Never mind," I said.

I didn't want Walter to go away to build houses and make roads. I wanted him to stay right here with me.

2
Gingersnaps

About once a week my teacher, Miss Rosalie Smith, would ask me to go to the store for her after school. As the other children left, she'd call me to her desk and take out her change purse. She'd count out a dollar or so and say, "One box of gingersnaps and one tin of tea. And here's a dime for you, Wanda."

Her mother and father were old, and she liked to bring gingersnaps and tea home to them.

I'd race down to Podorozny's Market, and after I bought the cookies and tea, I'd linger over the penny-candy counter with my dime. Sometimes I'd be tempted by the red licorice twists or the taffy, but I'd always end up getting a sack of peanuts. Peanuts were Walter's favorite, and I liked to share with him.

"Thank you for the dime, Miss Smith."

"Thank you for going to the store for me, Wanda," said my teacher, smiling at me.

"You're welcome, Miss Smith," I said.

"You're a good girl, Wanda. Polite like your brother, Walter."

Miss Rosalie Smith was wonderful, and I wanted to be a teacher just like her. She was smart and wore pretty dresses and beautiful high-heel shoes. That's what I would wear when I got to be a teacher.

I was always nagging at Ma to come to school to meet my teacher. But Ma would never come—I knew that. Still, I thought how wonderful it would be if she did.

I would say, "Ma, this is my teacher, Miss Smith. Miss Smith, this is my mother, Mrs. Malinski."

And they would like each other and have tea and gingersnaps together. I would be so proud.

"Ma, please come to school and meet my teacher.

You'll like her, and she'll like you. Please come," I'd beg.

"Get out," she'd say, laughing. "And which fancy-shmancy dress should I wear? This one?" And she'd point to the big hole at her waist where a button used to be. "Or that one?" And she'd point to the other dress hanging on the clothesline—the dress with the big grease stain on the stomach.

"You can wear your coat over it!" I'd say.

Ma still wore the same coat she had on when she came to America. The coat was old even then. Now it was worn through at the elbows, and it pouched and sagged all over.

"Get out!" she'd say, laughing.

"Oh, Ma . . ."

Even if Ma had fancy-shmancy, she still wouldn't have come to my school. The women on our street used to invite her to their houses. They'd knock on our door, but she never let them in. She'd make up some excuse about someone being sick. Sometimes she'd be out sweeping the stoop or hanging up the wash, and a neighbor would try to start a

conversation with her. But Ma would say supper was burning and come running in.

She sang a lot—songs about friends, about soldiers, and about angels and children. She'd cook, and she'd sing. She'd rock, and she'd sing. She'd sew, and she'd sing. And every time she sang the song about the angels and the children, she'd cry. Well, I guess it was a very sad song.

"Ma, you should make friends with the other ladies," I'd say. "You'd like them."

And that would make Ma cry more. "It's hard being in a new country. I'm not smart like you, Wanda. It's hard for me."

She could be so sad, and that made me sad, too. When I grew up, there would be gingersnaps for my ma.

3

Rats in the Cellar

Pa, why didn't you name me something pretty like Rosalie!" I pouted. "Why Wanda, Wanda, Wanda? Rosalie is so pretty."

"Okay, Rosalie, get down in the cellar and help your brother bring up some coal for the stove!" he said.

That was one of our jobs—Walter's and mine. I didn't like going down to the cellar alone. It was scary-dark and dirty and damp. Walter walked ahead of me, while I clung to his shirt.

"For heaven's sake, Wanda! Let go! My collar's choking me!"

"Look, Walter!" I gasped. "Look over there! There's a rat!"

We stood still on the stairs.

"I don't see anything. Are you sure?" he asked.

"Yes, yes!" I whispered. "I saw it!"

Suddenly two giant rats darted out from behind the potato sack. I screamed and ran to the top of the stairs. Walter was braver than I was. He grabbed a shovel and chased them until he cornered one of them near the coal bin.

Whack! Whack!

"What's going on down there?" Pa yelled.

Walter brought the dead rat upstairs for Pa to see.

"See, I told you there are rats down there!" he said to Pa angrily.

"Get that thing out of here! Get it out, wise guy!" Pa yelled at him.

Walter threw the rat outside in the trash barrel. When he came back in, he looked Pa straight in the eye and said, "I'll be glad when you send me

16

away to the CCC. There'll be no more shoveling cellar rats for me!"

Pa took the shovel and hit Walter in the bee-hind with it. From now on, Walter and I would keep our rats to ourselves.

4
Victoria

Victoria was lucky. She was eighteen and didn't have to help much around the house. She had a paying job! She did housework for Mrs. Harrington. Mrs. Harrington often gave Victoria leftovers to take home to us. Ham, roast beef, and even lamb! Mrs. Harrington used to give Victoria dresses she didn't want to wear anymore. Once she even took Victoria to New York and bought her a pair of high heels with bows!

The Harringtons were rich. Mr. Harrington was the owner of the cotton mill. They had a son Curtis who was my age. He was in my class at school, but I didn't have anything to do with him. Curtis was fresh and always got into trouble. The older son, Andrew Harrington, was a "super," or superintendent at the mill. He used to sneak home early to talk to Victoria before she left for the day. I think he was in love with her.

He took her roller-skating, and they went downtown to the movies every time a new one was playing. Andrew had a car and wore polished shoes and a necktie. Ma wanted Victoria to marry him. Ma said in America this could happen.

Victoria knew about everything. She fixed her hair in the latest style, and she knew all about the new dresses and hats. She knew every single word of the popular songs and sang right along when they were played on the radio.

She was a great dancer, too. She liked to practice with me so she'd look good when she went out with Andrew. She'd turn on the radio music, and we'd dance all around the kitchen.

Walter never wanted to join us. "Not me. I don't have dancing feet," he'd say.

Dancing was such fun. We'd twirl and kick and swing! We'd get to giggling and shrieking. Walter and Ma would get caught up in it. They'd laugh and shake their heads.

"Oh, you two!" Ma would say.

Pa didn't approve of dancing and music.

"Crazy stuff! You won't get ahead in life wasting your time like that!" Pa said.

Once Pa and Victoria had a big fight about her wearing lipstick, but Victoria wore it anyway. Pa let her get away with a lot because she had a paying job.

"If it weren't for Victoria, we'd be on relief," Pa said. That made Ma cry. The city gave out a little money to those who didn't have work.

One time Walter said, "It'll be better next year. I'll be sixteen and quit school and get a job."

"And what job will that be, wise guy?" Pa asked. "Who'll hire a stupid like you? Aah!"

Walter left the house and slammed the door.

"He's a good son," Ma said. "He wants to help. Don't talk to him like that."

Why did Pa have to be so mean? I stood at the window and watched my brother shuffling down the street. He kicked rocks. He kicked a trash can.

I wanted to open the window and yell, "Walter, you're a good son! You're a good son!"

Victoria joined me at the window. "Pa sure is hard on him. Pa's just like Walter—they both have a lot on their minds."

5
The Argument

Walter wasn't good in school. Oh, he was polite, but school was hard for him. He couldn't read too well. He'd get all the words mixed up and spell everything backward. And he never remembered his multipication tables. Walter had been held back twice.

But there was nobody like Walter when it came to cars. Fixing cars just came naturally to him. He learned a lot, too, by hanging around at City Service Garage. Often the mechanics asked him to help out. Sometimes he'd get paid and sometimes not. But Walter hung around just the same. He was hoping they'd take him on when times got better.

I wondered what would happen to those garage plans if Walter got into the CCC.

Pa and Cousin Chester went down to City Hall, and they filled out an application for Walter, lying about Walter's age, of course. The clerk said Walter had to sign it himself. There was a big argument that night. Ma said she didn't want Walter to go to no army camp.

"I told you! This is not an army camp!" Pa said. "He'll be making money. He'll be learning how to do something useful. What's he going to do—sit around here and be a bum?"

"Don't think you're making me go," Walter said. "I want to do a man's work. I am a man—the only one in this house!"

Pa went for him then, but Ma stood in front of Walter.

"Leave him alone! Leave him alone!" she screamed.

"Aah, you!" Pa yelled. "The day is coming, Walter! When you get your CCC letter from Roosevelt, you'll go. And you'll send home your money for your mother—the mother you make cry all the time!"

Walter signed the application form. Then he left the house without his coat and stayed out in the cold for a long, long time.

I wanted to rip up that paper and throw it in the stove. Victoria was right. Walter was too young to go. What if someone found out about the lie? Walter might get into trouble—with President Roosevelt. And Walter wasn't the one who made Ma cry. Didn't Pa know that?

6
Friends and Bullies

Ida was my best friend. Miss Rosalie Smith said we were like two peas in a pod. I was the best reader in our fifth-grade class—Ida was the best speller. Ida and I were tied for arithmetic.

There was only one time I ever got mad at Ida, and it was because of bratty Curtis Harrington, the mill owner's younger son. A bunch of us were walking to school together. There had been an ice storm the night before, and now it was raining. I had holes in my shoes, and I was trying to get to school as carefully as I could. It was no use, though. There were puddles everywhere. Every squishy step I took made the wad of paper in the bottom of each shoe as soppy as a sponge. Curtis came running by and deliberately shoved me into an enormous puddle.

"Ha! What are you doing, Wanda? Taking a bath?" Curtis laughed. "Wanda's taking a baaath!"

"You're a rotten, mean kid, Curtis!" I hollered. "But I'm not afraid of you!"

All the other kids were scared of him, and they didn't dare say or do anything.

Curtis didn't care about anyone or anything. He never had to worry about his shoes. He didn't have to wear hand-me-downs like I did. All he had to do was be rich and bratty. Curtis ran off, laughing.

I got up clumsily, and Ida put her arm around me. "I hate that Curtis!" Ida said.

I wasn't mad at her yet.

When we got to school, I hung up my wet coat. I almost started crying when I saw how wet my dress was, too. I went to my seat, and it wasn't long before I had dripped a big, dark puddle under my desk.

Curtis saw it and hollered out, "Wanda wet her paaants! Wanda wet her paaants!"

That's when everyone started laughing at me and pointing. Ida laughed, too! Thanks, Ida. That's when I got mad at her.

"Wanda wet her paaants!" Curtis said.

"I did not!" I hollered back.

Miss Rosalie Smith didn't like all this hollering.

"That's enough of that!" she said. "Wanda, come here."

I dripped my way up to her desk.

"What happened to you? You're soaked through."

"Curtis pushed me in a puddle on the way to school."

"Curtis, is that true? Did you do that?" she asked.

Curtis didn't answer. He was angrily chopping up his eraser with a ruler.

Ida was feeling guilty that she had laughed. "It's true, Miss Smith. We all saw him do it," she said. That's when I stopped being mad at Ida.

"Well, you'll stay after school, Curtis. You and I are going to have a long talk. Wanda, you come with me."

Miss Rosalie Smith took me into the coatroom and made me take off my dress. She put it on the radiator so it would dry. Ida let me borrow her coat.

As I walked back to my seat, Curtis hissed at me. "You just wait, Wanda! I'll get even with you!"

7

The Doctor's Guide

On my birthday, when I woke up, I could smell the cabbage soup Ma had already started on the stove. Ma was a good cook.

"You should open a restaurant, Ma," I said. "A little luncheonette. You could do the cooking, and I'd wait on the people. We could make lots of money! You could be famous, Ma!"

"Get out," she said.

"Mmmm . . . I love your kapusta, Ma." I hugged her.

"Good, because you're going to eat it all week." That was okay with me.

"What's the birthday girl going to do today?" she

asked me. It was Saturday, and I had the whole day free.

"Oh, I don't know. I'll probably go to Ida's house. She has a present for me."

Ida had promised me a pin with a little dog on it that she won last year in a spelling bee.

And Victoria was bringing me a surprise from the Harringtons'. Just as long as it wasn't Curtis!

"You bring Ida home with you later," Ma said. "She can have some soup with us."

Ida and I met Pa on the way back to our house. He was carrying a big box.

"Hey, Rosalie, I got a birthday present for you!" Pa said.

"What is it? Tell me!" I wasn't expecting anything.

"You'll see."

We all went into the house. Pa dropped the box on the floor. "See! Books! Just what you like, Rosalie!"

Ida and I sat beside the box, taking out one book at a time. Walter came to see, too.

"You got books?" Ma said. "Where did you get them?"

"Downtown at the library. I was walking by, and I saw some men carrying out these boxes and putting them by the curb. I was looking in the boxes, and a fella said, 'Hey, you want 'em? Take 'em.' They were cleaning out a storage room. Old books. Happy birthday, Wanda."

"Thank you, Pa." I wanted to hug him, but no one ever hugged Pa. He didn't let us.

Victoria came home a little while later. She brought me half a chocolate cake. We cut it up into small pieces for everyone. This was the best birthday I'd ever had.

Later, Ida, Walter, and I sat on Walter's cot in the corner of the kitchen and took a good look at my books. There was a book of Shakespeare plays. It was hard to read. I didn't understand much of it, but I knew Shakespeare was supposed to be important. There was an algebra book, too. Maybe I'd like that when I was older. There was a book with stories about famous rich men. That was interesting. But the most interesting book was one

called *Doctor's Guide*. It had naked bodies in it and pictures of all sorts of warts and rashes. Pa couldn't read much English. He couldn't have known what the books were about.

Pa heard us giggling and came over to us. I slapped the book shut.

"You like those books, don't you?" he asked.

"Yes, Pa. Thank you."

"Good. Read, read." Pa smiled.

8
Walter's Present

Monday after school, Walter insisted I go to Podorozny's Market with him. He wanted to buy me a present. "Just a little something," he said.

"But, Walter, you're saving your garage money for new shoes," I said.

"So, I can buy you just a little something for your birthday. Besides, they'll give me good shoes when they take me at the CCC."

I didn't want any candy. I'd rather Walter got himself some new shoes. But I wanted Walter to feel good, so I went with him.

"Look, they've got red licorice. Get that. You like it," Walter said.

We were leaning over the candy counter, and I was having trouble making up my mind.

"Get what you want. It's for you," he said.

That's when Anna Podorozny came over to wait on us. Anna-with-the-dimples. "What can I get for you?" she asked, giving Walter a big smile.

"She's still looking," Walter answered. "It's her birthday."

"How sweet! You're treating!" Anna said.

"She's still looking," Walter said again.

"Take as long as you want, Wanda. I haven't seen you in a while, Walter. How have you been?"

"Busy. I've been helping out down at Bob's City Service. Helping out."

"Oh, Walter, you must be quite a mechanic for Bob to take you on," Anna squealed.

"I'm pretty good."

"You know, there's a dance at the church Saturday night. I'm going. Are you going to be there?"

"No, I don't think so."

"Aw, why not, Walter?" she asked. "A lot of kids go. Father Dankewicz chaperones. We all have fun. It's a church dance."

39

Walter shook his head. "No."

"Say you'll come," she begged. That smile again. "I'll teach you how to dance, Walter. I know you'll be good at it."

"Oh, I know how to dance!"

Walter! I couldn't take much more of this. Anna was boy-crazy—that's what Ma would say. I thought it was disgusting.

"I can't go. I have to work. Bob's City Service— he's paying me to work Saturdays now."

I turned to him. "Walter! I didn't know you got a job! That's wonderful!" Why hadn't he told me this great news?

"Yes, well, I do!" Walter kicked me.

"Ow! Ow!" I cried.

"What's the matter with her?" Anna asked, looking at me.

"I'm sick. I have a pain in my stomach. Let's go, Walter," I said.

"Well, here. Take this for later," Anna said, handing me two red licorice sticks. "A present."

"No, I'm buying," Walter said. He paid, and we left.

"Come back real soon, Walter."

When we got down to the corner, I stopped and looked Walter in the eye.

"Well, do you have a job, or don't you?" I asked.

"Wanda, you're smart, but sometimes you're dumb," he said. But he wasn't mad at me.

When we got home, Walter lay on his mattress in the kitchen and listened to the radio. Roosevelt was talking about the CCC again. After a while, Walter turned the radio off.

"Walter, keep it on. *The Lone Ranger* will be on soon," I said.

"So, I don't care about the radio tonight."

He lay staring at the ceiling.

I showed him yesterday's newspaper that Victoria had brought us from the Harringtons'.

"Walter, there's a big story about that baseball star, Lou Gehrig. Here's the sports page—see?"

"Later. I'm thinking."

I didn't like his worried look.

"What are you thinking about?" I asked.

"Just thinking."

I gave up. I went to my bedroom—mine and Vic-

41

toria's. She wasn't home yet, so I pulled out the books Pa had given me. I tried to figure out some of the algebra stuff, but I got really confused. I took out the *Doctor's Guide* instead.

9

Rotten Fruit

Pa was hollering.

"Yes! You're going!"

"Pa, please. It's not dark yet," Walter said.

"You go now!"

Pa used to send us down to the market to ask for oranges or whatever Podorozny was throwing out. Podorozny would let us pile the stuff in our wagon, and we'd hurry home with it. We'd cut the spoiled parts off, of course, before we ate anything.

"Pa, I hate going there begging for rotten fruit! I feel like dirt!"

"You go, or we'll be eating dirt!" Pa said. "We do what we have to do!"

"Well, you go beg! You're the man of the house!"

Pa looked like he'd been slapped.

Suddenly Pa's hand flew across Walter's face. Walter touched his stinging cheek. His eyes filled with tears.

"Pa!" I gasped.

Pa glared at Walter. "You do as you're told! You go now!"

"I'll go, Pa," I said. "Let me go instead."

Ma put her hand gently on Walter's shoulder. "Do what your father says," she whispered.

Walter choked back sobs, and big tears rolled down his face. He put on his jacket.

"Wait for me, Walter. I'll go with you," I said. I reached for my coat, but he was already out the door.

Ma turned to Pa. "I don't like what's happening in this family," she said. "I know it's hard for you not having a job, but he's your son. Don't treat him like that."

That night I prayed for Pa to get a job. I prayed

for Pa to be nice to Walter. I prayed for Walter to never have to go away to the CCC. I prayed for Walter to have a friend like I had Ida. I prayed for Walter to learn to dance.

10
The Penknife

That week we had a cold snap. It was the kind of cold that stung your nose and chapped your lips as soon as you got outside. Our wet laundry froze right on the clothesline. When Ma brought in Pa's pants, they stood up all by themselves. We had to hang the laundry on a clothesline Ma strung across the kitchen.

Walter and I had to make several trips down to the cellar for coal, and Pa sent us to pick up coal near the train tracks. Sometimes coal would fall off the trains, and we could fill our wagon. Ma always warned us to be careful, but Walter liked to do dangerous things. Sometimes he would stay right on the tracks when a train was coming. The engineer would blow the whistle, and I'd scream and beg him to get away. And then he'd jump clear just at the last minute.

"I know what I'm doing. Don't go crazy," he'd say.

We were walking along the tracks, sharing the peanuts I'd bought that day with Miss Rosalie Smith's dime.

"You're going to be a teacher someday," Walter said.

"Maybe," I answered.

"You will. You're smart."

I grinned.

"You'll be a teacher just like Miss Rosalie Smith. You'll win a scholarship or something. You'll even wear high heels."

I grinned. "Get out."

"Miss Wanda Malinski. That's what the kids will call you. Miss Wanda Malinski."

"Stop teasing, Walter!" I said. I gave him a little shove. He gave me a push and ran ahead.

I chased after him. "You're going to get it, Walter!"

"Miss Wanda Malinski runs like a chicken!"

Then Walter stopped and picked up something shiny. I caught up with him.

"What's that?"

"A penknife. Not too rusty, either. I could use a penknife."

We were standing there examining the knife when Curtis Harrington and two other boys came running up the slope. The two boys were wearing matching knitted hats. I didn't know their names—they weren't in our class—but I'd seen them at school.

"Hey! What you cockroaches got there in that stupid wagon?" Curtis said. He stood kicking rocks up our way. The two Hats poked each other and snickered.

"Hey, cockroaches! Answer me!"

"Shut up, Harrington!" Walter said.

"Scram, ugly!" I yelled.

"Yeah, and you got a big mouth, Wanda! You like to tell on kids at school. You're a tattletale!" Curtis said.

He skimmed a rock at me. I picked up a piece of

coal and threw it at him. It smacked him in the nose. Curtis came at me and knocked me down. Walter pushed him. Then Curtis kicked me when I tried to get up. The Hats started coming at me, too. That's when Walter jumped in front of them with the penknife.

"Get out of here, Harrington. You're nothing but a bullyboy who picks on girls."

"Oh, yeah?" Curtis said.

Walter reached out with the knife as if he was going to cut Curtis's jacket.

"Hey, quit it!" Curtis said. He was scared. The Hats were nervous, too.

"Get out of here right now, Harrington! Take your ugly face and your ugly friends and get out!" Walter said.

Curtis and the two other boys turned and ran. Curtis tripped on the tracks and fell down, splitting his pants.

We all laughed. We could see his underwear! We laughed harder and harder—even the Hats laughed. Curtis had a big bee-hind, and I always knew someday he'd split his britches.

Walter and I went back to coal picking, and every now and then one of us would burst out laughing at the thought of Curtis sprawled across the tracks with his underwear showing.

11
Police

Walter was loading the stove with coal, and Pa was sitting in the rocking chair, trying to read the newspaper.

"Come here, Wanda. What's this word?"

"That's 'economic,'" I said.

"And what's this?"

"That says 'government predictions.'"

"You're smart, Wanda. You're gonna be somebody," Pa said. I smiled inside. I liked when Pa said things like that to me.

The knock at the door was loud and urgent. Ma and I were startled and almost spilled the bowls of cabbage soup we were carrying to the supper table.

"Who is it?" Pa called out.

"Police. We need to talk to you."

Pa hurried to the door and unlocked it. "Yes, sir?" he asked.

"Are you Mr. Malinski?"

"Yes, sir," Pa answered.

Pa stood aside as the two officers entered. It was crowded in our kitchen. A clothesline with our wet laundry was strung across the room, and it made the room even smaller. The policemen had to duck under the laundry as they came in. The tall one turned to his partner and smirked.

"Mr. Malinski, do you have a son named Walter?" the other officer asked.

"Yes, sir. I do," Pa answered. "Why? What is it?"

Walter moved to Pa's side.

"Are you Walter?" the officer said.

"Yes, sir." Walter looked scared. We were all scared.

"Mr. Malinski," the policeman said. "There was an incident down by the railroad tracks this afternoon. Curtis Harrington says your son Walter attacked him with a knife."

"My son has no knife!" Pa said.

"What? What?" Ma asked, grabbing my arm.

"My son has no knife!" Pa insisted.

Walter reddened.

"Do you have a knife?" the policeman asked.

"Yes, sir. I do," my brother answered.

"Go get it, then," the policeman said.

Walter went to his cot and took the penknife out from under his mattress. Pa's eyes flashed. I could hear his short, hard breath.

"Where did you get that? Where?" Pa demanded.

Ma was yammering in Polish, and I had to shush her.

Walter handed the penknife to the policeman.

"You're very lucky, Mr. Malinski. Curtis Harrington's father is a very important man in this town, and he has agreed not to press charges if we confiscate the knife."

Then the officer spoke again to Walter. "You'd better wise up, kid. There are laws in this country. You can't go around attacking people with knives."

I saw the look on Walter's face. I saw the look on

Pa's face. I couldn't restrain myself any longer. I grabbed Pa's arm.

"Pa, Walter didn't attack anyone. I was there. I know!"

Pa shoved me away. "Shut up, Wanda! Shut up!" he yelled. He shoved me away.

"Mr. Malinski, you'd better teach your children right from wrong," the policeman went on. "This is America. You're in America now."

"Yes, sir. Yes, sir," Pa answered.

The two policemen turned to leave and ducked back under the laundry. I heard the tall one say, "How can they live like this? It smells like something died in here!" I hated cabbage soup from that day on.

As the policemen left our house, the crowd of curious neighbors parted to let them pass. Pa went to the window and pulled down the shade.

Then he turned to Walter. "You! You! You bring police to this family! You bring shame to this family!" And he took his belt off and hit Walter over and over again.

"Pa, don't! Pa!" I pleaded.

"Stop! Stop!" Ma cried.

Pa opened the cellar door and pushed Walter down into the dark. "A rat! That's what you are! Sleep with the rats!" Pa slammed the door.

"Let's eat!" he said to Ma and me.

We sat down with our bread and our soup. I didn't want to eat. I never wanted to eat again. I put my head in my hands and sobbed.

"Eat!" Pa said, pounding the table.

I pushed my chair back and ran to my room. I threw myself on the bed and wept.

Some time later Ma came into my room with a hunk of bread. "Here. For you and Walter. Go give it to him."

I went into the kitchen and glanced at Pa sitting with the newspaper. He said nothing.

When I opened the cellar door, Ma said, "Tell Walter to come up. My son does not sleep with rats!" She glared at Pa. He said nothing.

When Victoria came home from the Harringtons', she took Walter outside for a talk. It was late when they returned, and I saw her hug Walter. She came into our room and put on her nightgown and got under the covers. She was crying.

"What's the matter?" I asked.

"I don't know if I ever want to be related to Curtis Harrington," she said.

A couple of weeks later, there was a lot of excitement at school. Everyone was talking about it. It was in the newspaper, too. Podorozny's Market had been robbed!

Mr. Podorozny and his family were asleep in their tenement above the market when they heard the loud crash of glass breaking. Mr. Podorozny ran downstairs in his long johns and confronted a boy stealing money from the cash register. It was the rich boy, Curtis Harrington, stealing! Curtis tried to run away, but Mr. Podorozny stopped him with a broom and held him until the police arrived. The police put Curtis in the paddy wagon and took him to the station. Mr. Harrington had to come down to get him. He offered Mr. Podorozny a lot of money to settle up, but Mr. Podorozny wanted to press charges. He said Curtis was a rotten kid who needed to learn a lesson. Victoria heard Mr. and Mrs. Harrington talking about sending Curtis away to boarding school.

Ma said Curtis was turning out bad probably because his father hollered at him too much. Pa said maybe Curtis was turning out bad because his mother was too softhearted. But Victoria said, from what she saw, no one paid any attention to Curtis at all.

12
Sirens

The weather was warming up. The snow was starting to get slushy. "Today will be our last good sledding day," Walter said.

Walter and I hurried home from school that afternoon and took off with our old sled. Our favorite spot was the big hill behind the cotton mill.

"Be careful," Ma said. "You never know."

The river ran right by the cotton mill, and Ma worried that we'd fall in.

Walter did dangerous things.

It was getting dark. We had stayed too late, and we'd be in trouble when we got home. We were taking a shortcut through the mill yard. It was

spooky. No one worked nights anymore, and there were only a few lights on outside the mill. Walter stopped to skim some rocks over the ice on the river. That's when we spotted something sticking out of the ice.

"It looks like a suitcase!" Walter said.

"Oh, it's probably an old lunch bag!" I said.

"No. I bet it's a suitcase, and there might be money in it. Maybe some bank robbers were being chased and they got scared and threw the bag of money in the river."

"Walter, it looks like a lunch bag. Someone from the mill probably lost it, and there's a moldy salami sandwich in it. Come on. Let's go."

"No, I'm going to try to get it. If there's money in there, I can give it to Pa, and I won't have to go to CCC."

"I thought you wanted to go to CCC."

Walter pushed the sled out onto the icy river. "See, the ice didn't crack at all. It's still frozen enough to walk on."

"Come on, Walter. I'm cold. Please—let's go home. It's dangerous to play here."

"Who's playing? All I'm going to do is get the suitcase."

I grabbed his jacket. "No, Walter. Let's go."

"Here. You hold the rope. If the ice starts to crack, I can hang on to the sled and you can pull me off."

"I want to go home. Please, Walter."

"Don't go crazy! I know what I'm doing!"

Walter stepped cautiously onto the ice and made it to the suitcase. He began yanking on the handle.

"This thing is really stuck!"

He pulled again and fell backward onto the ice.

There was a loud crack. The ice opened up, and Walter fell through into the cold, dark water.

"Walter! Walter!" I screamed.

He clutched at the edge of the broken ice. "Help me, Wanda! Help me!" he called.

"Grab the sled! The sled, Walter!"

"I can't reach it! Help me! The water's cold! I'm so cold!"

And before I could do anything, he went down. He went down, and I couldn't even see him.

"Walter! Walter!"

Oh, God, no! No!

"Walter!" I yelled. "Walter!"

There was no answer. Walter was somewhere in the freezing water under the ice.

I raced through the mill yard. I ran past the school. Finally, I reached Bob's City Service. Thank God the mechanic was still there, working late. Wild and breathless, I burst into the garage.

"Oh, no! Not Walter!" Bob said. "You stay right here."

Bob ran to the fire station, and in seconds the bells were clanging and the sirens screaming. The police and the fire department were on their way. Bob put me in his car and sped to my house.

"Walter fell through the ice! Walter's drowning!" he told Pa. Then both of them jumped into Bob's car and raced to the river.

Drowning? He wasn't drowning! He just fell through the ice! Drowning means dying! "Walter's not drowning!" I told myself.

Ma and Victoria and I prayed all night.

It was after midnight when Pa came home with Bob. We knew before they even said the words. Bob told us.

"Walter's dead. He drowned. The firemen found him." Then he broke down and cried.

Pa slumped into the rocking chair and bawled as I never imagined a man could bawl. It was scary. Ma ran to him and put her head in his lap, and they cried together.

"My Walter! My Walter is dead," Pa wailed. "Walter, Walter. Walter."

Pa loved you, Walter, and you never knew it. You never knew.

A broken heart hurts so much. Worse than a dizzy headache and a sick stomach and a bad note from the teacher and your best friend being mad at you all at once. Worse than that. Much worse. How could things change so fast? One afternoon I was having fun on a sled with my brother—both of us laughing and rolling in the snow. Then an hour later there were sirens screeching, and rescue wagons speeding through the streets, and everyone searching for my brother in the cold, dark river. How could things change so fast?

There'd be no CCC for Walter Malinski. No garage job. No dances with Anna. A broken heart hurts so much.

13
The Visitors

The week after the funeral, we had a lot of visitors. Women on our street came by with all kinds of food. Father Dankewicz came with some church people, too.

"Here, Wanda, give this to your mother."

"You're a good daughter. We're praying for your family."

One day Mr. Podorozny and Anna came by. Mr. Podorozny brought us a whole box of groceries.

"Tell your ma and pa if they need anything, just send down."

"Here, Wanda. For you," Anna said. She gave

me a big sack of penny candy. I didn't even want it, but I took it because I could tell she felt bad.

It was like a dream. And I was there, but I wasn't. It was like I was sick with the flu, and I wanted my mother to take care of me. But she couldn't. Nobody could. Everyone was too sick to take care of anyone else.

After the funeral, Pa went to the cellar and stayed there. Victoria cooked his food and took it down to him. Ma would get up every morning and sit in the rocking chair by the stove, and Victoria would make her a cup of tea. Ma would rock and sing. She'd sing that song about angels and children and then cry and cry.

Victoria would turn on the radio. "Ma, let's hear some music. Listen—it's Benny Goodman's Orchestra! You like him."

"No, no radio today."

Then Ma would shuffle back to the bedroom for the rest of the day. After a while, she didn't bother getting out of bed at all.

Victoria stayed home mornings with us, and af-

ternoons she went to work at the Harringtons'
house. She'd leave me with chores to do—awful
chores. Wash the woodwork. Scrub the bathroom.
Iron the clothes. Make three or four trips to the
cellar for coal. I'd pass Pa on the stairs. He'd be sitting there with his head in his hands, just looking
at nothing in the dark.

"Come up, Pa," I'd say.

He wouldn't answer.

"I smell whiskey in the cellar," I told Victoria.

"There's no whiskey. You don't even know what
whiskey smells like," Victoria said.

It smelled like whiskey to me.

"You have to go back to school," Victoria said one
morning. She was cutting noodles out of the dough
she'd just rolled.

"No!" I said. I didn't want the kids to look at me
funny. I was afraid they would treat me funny. I
didn't want anyone looking at me like that. "No!"

"Yes, you have to go back! It's time."

"No!" I said.

"Listen, if you don't go to school, the truant of-

ficer will come get me and put me in jail. Then who will support this family? Well?"

"Leave me alone!" I said. "Are you the boss lady now?"

"I have enough to cope with!" she yelled at me. "I don't need a fresh-mouth sister giving me trouble!"

"I can't go, Victoria. Please," I pleaded.

Victoria bowed her head, and I saw tears roll down her cheeks. "I can't take any more of this. He was my Walter, too." Then she started flinging noodles all over the place. "I can't take any more of this!" she shrieked.

Noodles stuck to the clock. They hung from the window shades. They clung to my clean woodwork. Then she threw the heavy mixing bowl against the wall, and the bowl broke in half. She ripped off her apron and fled to the bedroom.

I heard her slamming bureau drawers, and in a little while she came out very dressed up. She was wearing the high heels Mrs. Harrington bought for her. She stomped across the kitchen, squashing noodles under her new shoes. She left, shutting the door hard behind her.

I looked around the kitchen and sighed. Noodles everywhere. I bent down and started cleaning up the mess.

Some time later Victoria returned with Father Dankewicz and Pa's cousin Chester. I was glad I had cleaned up the kitchen. The two men went downstairs to talk to Pa.

Suddenly there was a lot of shouting in the cellar. Pa was getting louder and louder.

"Calm down. Calm down," Chester said.

Next there was a big crash! Victoria and I ran down the stairs. Chester was sprawled on the floor.

"Pa! Pa!" I screamed. I grabbed Pa's arm. He tried to shake me off as I clung to him.

Father Dankewicz put his hand on Pa's shoulder. "Mr. Malinski, we're here to help," he said. "Let us help you." He nodded at me. "Please let us help you and your family."

Pa looked down at me and then covered his face with his hands. He stood quietly and sighed.

"Take her, Victoria," he said. "Go upstairs."

"You come, too, Pa," I begged.

"Go on, Wanda," Chester said. "We'll talk with your pa. Everything will be all right."

Victoria led me away and got me started washing the dishes.

After a while, Father Dankewicz and Chester came up. They had Pa with them! Pa washed and changed, and the three of them left the house. Pa came back just before supper. He was smiling.

"I have a job," he said. "I have a job, Rosalie!"

Walter's friend Bob at City Service had hired Pa to help fix cars. "I have a job!"

14
Chicken Soup

The next afternoon after Victoria and Pa left for work, there was a knock at the door. It was my best, best friend Ida, and her mother was with her. I liked Ida's mother. She always made me laugh. I offered Ida's mother a cup of tea.

"No, thanks," she said. She handed me a heavy bag. There was a plucked chicken in it!

Ida took her coat off.

"This is all yours!" She stacked my spelling book, my arithmetic book, and my geography book on the table. "Miss Smith wrote down all the pages for you to read and do. Here's paper, too. You missed a lot, you know!"

Ida and I sat on Walter's cot with the sack of candy Anna had given me. "You pick first," I said. I was glad she had come. "You're my best, best friend, Ida."

Ida's mother peered into Ma's bedroom.

"Well, look at you. You look awful," she said. "This is me speaking—Pani Lowicz. It's time you got out of bed and took care of your family."

"Leave me alone," Ma said.

Ida's mother came back into the kitchen.

"Get me your best pot, Wanda," she ordered in a loud voice. "I'm making chicken soup! I make the best chicken soup. Everybody says so. After you taste mine, you won't ever want anybody else's!" She winked at me.

I took her into the pantry. She started running water and chopping onions and banging utensils. Chop! Clang! Chop! Clang!

Suddenly Ma appeared in the kitchen. "What are you doing!" she demanded.

Mrs. Lowicz stepped into the room, and Ma grabbed the pot out of her hands.

"Nobody uses my pots but me!" Ma said.

"Okay. You peel the carrots, too," Mrs. Lowicz said.

Ida and I heard soft crying from the pantry. "I know. I know," Mrs. Lowicz said. "It'll get better. You'll be all right."

15

The School Picture

The next morning I left for school early, so I could get there before the other kids. I went right into my classroom. I didn't want anyone in the schoolyard to stand around looking at me funny.

Miss Rosalie Smith was correcting papers at her desk. I came in quietly and stood near the coatroom. She looked up.

"Wanda," she said. "I'm glad you're back."

I turned and started to leave. I wasn't ready for this. I'd never be ready.

"Wanda," she called, chasing after me. "Wanda."

She led me to her desk. "I have something for

you." She handed me a picture. It was a group picture of a class she once had. It was a picture of Walter. And he was smiling. Walter was looking right at me—and he was smiling.

From that day on, Ida and I walked home from school together. Sometimes she would stop at my house, because that's where her mother would be. Sometimes I would stop at her house, because that's where my mother would be. The two mothers got together almost every afternoon now. They were knitting us matching red sweaters. Ida and I were going to be the Sweaters!

16
Walter

Pa did well at City Service. He was a fast learner, and Bob liked him. The customers took to him, too. Pa made good money. We had meat and potatoes for supper every night. On his way home, Pa would stop at Podorozny's to buy fresh fruit. Soon he had saved enough money to buy all of us new shoes. Pa bought black lace-up shoes.

I showed Ma some beautiful toeless high heels. "Ooh, look, Ma! For you!"

"Get out!" she said, laughing.

Ma bought black lace-up shoes.

I begged her to let me try on some pretty red

shoes with bows. But I got black lace-up shoes, too. Maybe someday . . .

One evening Pa sat in the rocking chair studying a piece of paper. I stood by him and looked over his shoulder. He was looking at the application for the Civilian Conservation Corps. He stroked the place where Walter had signed it. He touched it again. Then he sighed. I kissed his cheek and gave him a big hug. And he let me.

It was odd how things worked out. It was terrible, terrible when Walter died. And then, after a while, all the good things started happening to us. It would have been better if Walter had been here to know all the good things, too. But maybe he did know. I could picture him sitting with the angels, listening to Ma singing, and smiling down on us. Setting things up and making sure only good things happened to me and Victoria and Ma and Pa. Someday, when I have children of my own, I'll tell them all about Walter.

"Once I had a brother named Walter. He made

me laugh, and he bought me birthday presents, and he protected me from bullies. He was proud of me, and he wanted me to be a teacher. But he was the real teacher. Once I had a brother named Walter, and he was the best brother in America."